The Juggli
by Glyn G

© THE MEDICI SOCIETY LIMITED 1992
Printed in England. ISBN 0 85503 173 5

Panda loves juggling

He practises all the time

Poor Frog and Tortoise!

They have to mend . . . . .

all the crockery

Yippee!!

Time to go swimming!

Oh dear . . .

more mending

and . . . *more* juggling

Ready at last!

Off they go

Panda juggling

plip! plip! plip!

Frog hopping

boing!   boing!   boing!

and Tortoise walking . . .

...very slowly

too slowly!

Wh . . . Whoo . . .

. . . o o o o o o ooops!

S...P... L...

A...S...H...!

but nothing has broken!

and Panda can practise

as much as he likes!